Monsters Love Colors. Copyright © 2013 by Mike Austin. All rights reserved. Manufactured in China. No part of this book may be used or reproduced in any manner whatsoever without written permission except in the case of brief quotations embodied in critical articles and reviews. For information address HarperCollins Children's Books, a division of HarperCollins Publishers, 10 East 53rd Street, New York, NY 10022. www.harpercollinschildrens.com. Library of Congress Cataloging-in-Publication Data is available.

ISBN 978-0-06-212594-1 (trade bdg.).

Typography by Mike Austin and Megan Stitt. The artist used his favorite monster pencils, monster crayons, monster ink and brushes, a scanner, and Adobe Photoshop to create the illustrations for this book. 12 13 14 15 16 SCP 10 9 8 7 6 5 4 3 2 1 ❖ First Edition

For Tien and Reid, my two little monsters —M.A.

MONSTERS LOVE COLORS

Written and Illustrated by

Mike Austin

HARPER

An Imprint of HarperCollinsPublishers

Monsters **love** to
scribble,
scribble,

mix,
dance,
and wiggle!

Mix,
mash,
and splash!

Squish, mish, and squash!

Squish!
Squash!
Mish!
Mash!

Mash!
Mish!
Squish!
Squash!

Monsters love new colors!

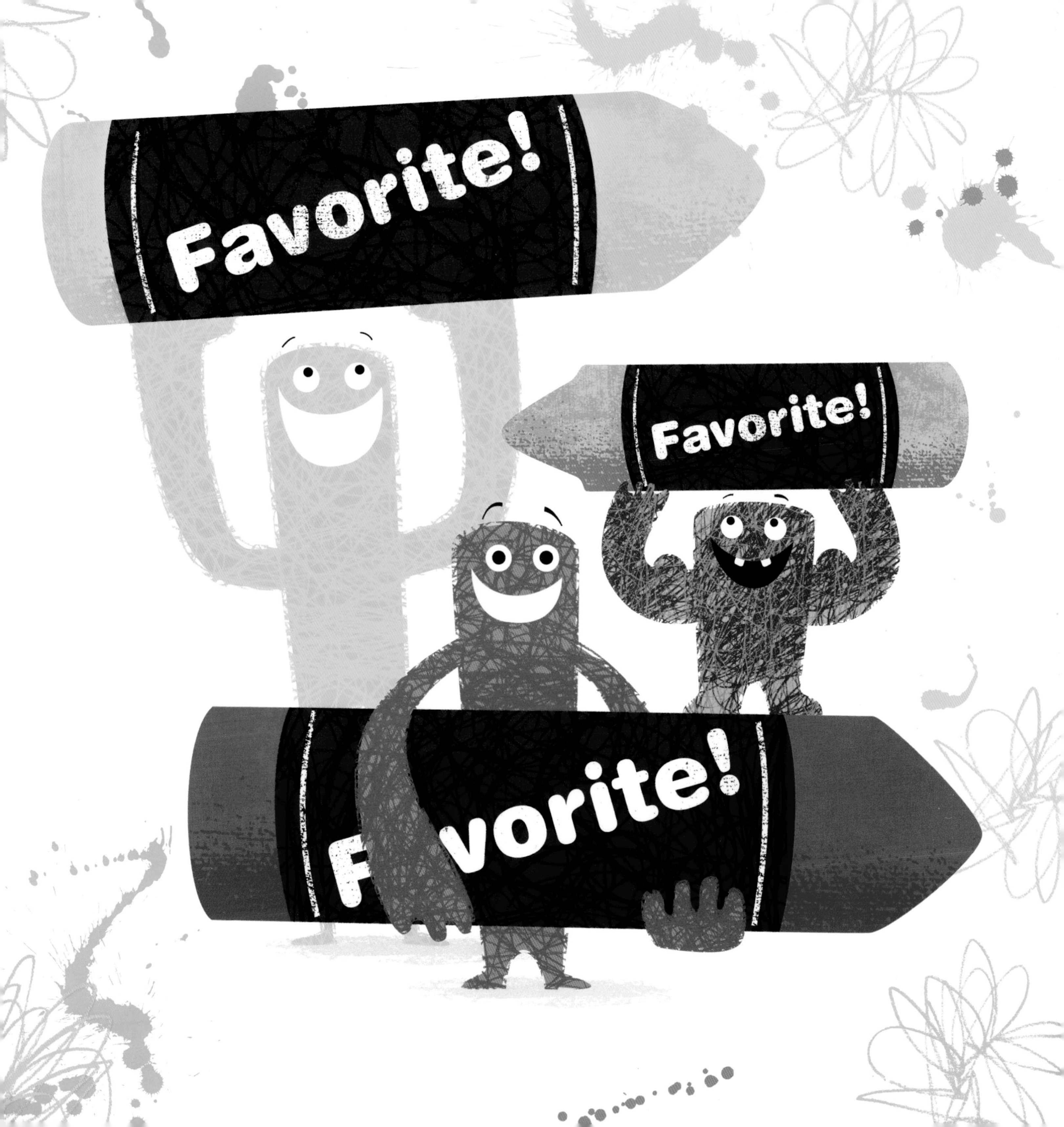
Favorite!
Favorite!
F vorite!

My favorite color is RED!

Red is the color of

ROAR!

and

SNORE!

and

More! More!

MORE!

RED!

My favorite color is
YELLOW!

Yellow is the color of

HOOOWWL!

PROWL!

and

HOWL!

and

GROWL! GROWL! GROWL! GROWL!

YELLOW!

My favorite color is

BLUE!

Blue is the color of

Scribble

and

Dribble

and

Nibble Nibble **Nibble**

Hey! Don't eat your
crayons, silly monster!

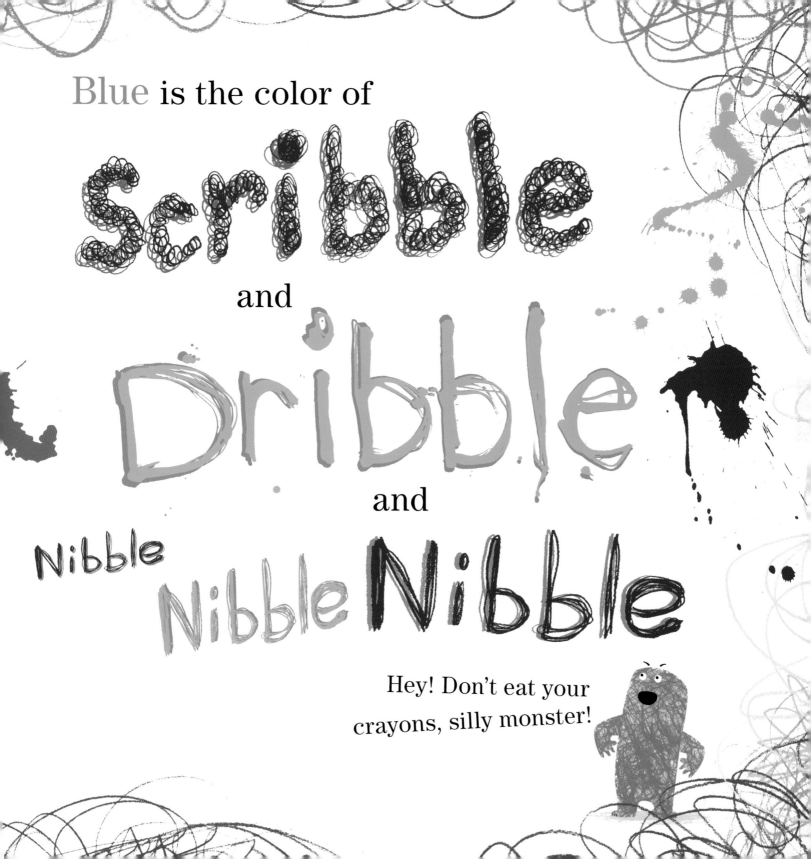

What new favorite color can we make for you?

ORANGE!

ORANGE!

Scribble, scribble, mix, dance, and wiggle!

Mixing red and yellow makes ORANGE!

And what new favorite color can we make for **you**?

Dribble! Scribble! Mix, dance, and wiggle!

Me next!

Mixing yellow and blue makes GREEN!

And what new favorite color can we make for **you**?

PURPLE!

Hey, buddy! *I* was
supposed to say
PURPLE!

Scribble, scribble, mix, dance, and wiggle!

Mixing red and blue makes PURPLE!

And what new favorite color
can we make for you?

Red?

Yellow?

Blue?

Orange?

Green?

Purple?

Hmmmmmmmmmm…

I know!

Monsters
love
new
colors!

Orange

Green

Purple

Rainbow!